A Note on Endangered Species

We are losing our animals. More than 5,000 animal species are endangered or threatened worldwide. This means that they are in danger of disappearing forever.

To safeguard these animals, there are over 3,500 protected areas in the form of parks, wildlife refuges and other reserves around the world. This book features ten of these endangered or threatened species.

We can all help save them by spreading the word about conservation.

The author wishes to thank Michael Sampson for his help in the preparation of this text.

PUFFIN BOOKS

Published by the Penguin Group
Penguin Books Ltd, 80 Strand, London WC2R 0RL, England
Penguin Group (USA) Inc., 375 Hudson Street, New York, New York 10014, USA
Penguin Group (Canada), 90 Eglinton Avenue East, Suite 700, Toronto, Ontario, Canada M4P 2Y3 (a division of Pearson Penguin Canada Inc.)
Penguin Ireland, 25 St Stephen's Green, Dublin 2, Ireland (a division of Penguin Books Ltd)
Penguin Group (Australia), 250 Camberwell Road, Camberwell, Victoria 3124, Australia (a division of Pearson Australia Group Pty Ltd)
Penguin Books India Pvt Ltd, 11 Community Centre, Panchsheel Park, New Delhi - 110 017, India
Penguin Group (NZ), 67 Apollo Drive, Rosedale, North Shore 0632, New Zealand (a division of Pearson New Zealand Ltd)
Penguin Books (South Africa) (Pty) Ltd, 24 Sturdee Avenue, Rosebank, Johannesburg 2196, South Africa

Penguin Books Ltd, Registered Offices: 80 Strand, London WC2R 0RL, England

puffinbooks.com

First published in the USA by Henry Holt and Company, LLC, 2003
Published in Great Britain in Puffin Books 2003
This edition published 2007
10 9 8 7 6 5 4 3

Text copyright © Bill Martin Jr, 2003
Illustrations copyright © Eric Carle, 2003
All rights reserved

The moral right of the author and illustrator has been asserted

Made and printed in China

British Library Cataloguing in Publication Data
A CIP catalogue record for this book is available from the British Library

ISBN: 978-0-141-50145-1

Panda Bear, Panda Bear, What Do You See?

By Bill Martin Jr
Pictures by Eric Carle

PUFFIN

Panda Bear,
Panda Bear,
what do you see?

I see a bald eagle
soaring by me.

Bald Eagle,
Bald Eagle,
what do you see?

I see a water buffalo
charging by me.

Water Buffalo,
Water Buffalo,
what do you see?

I see a spider monkey
swinging by me.

Spider Monkey,
Spider Monkey,
what do you see?

I see a green sea turtle
swimming by me.

Green Sea Turtle,
Green Sea Turtle,
what do you see?

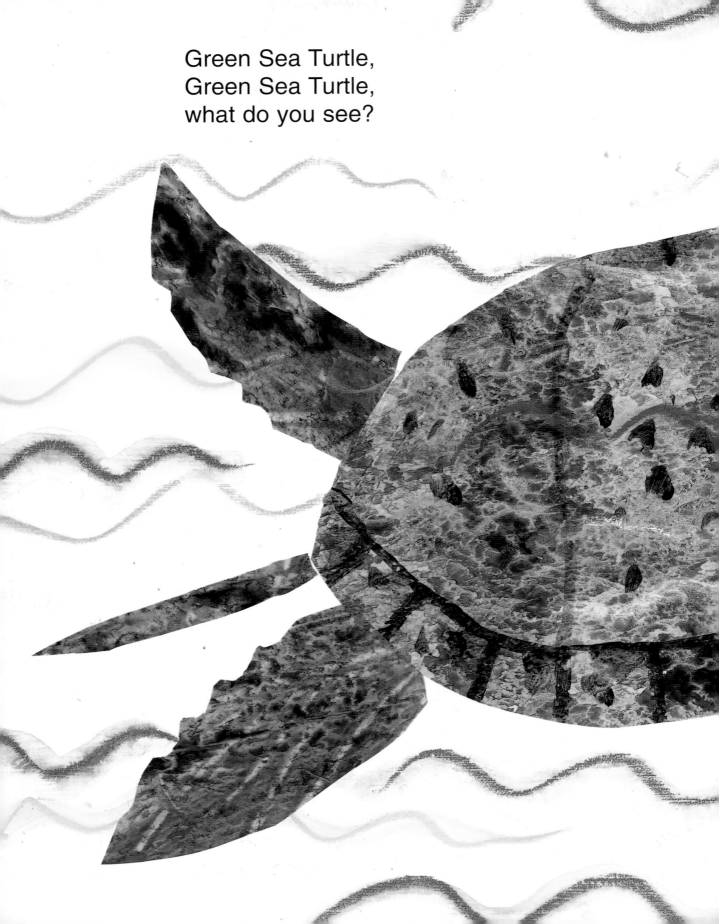

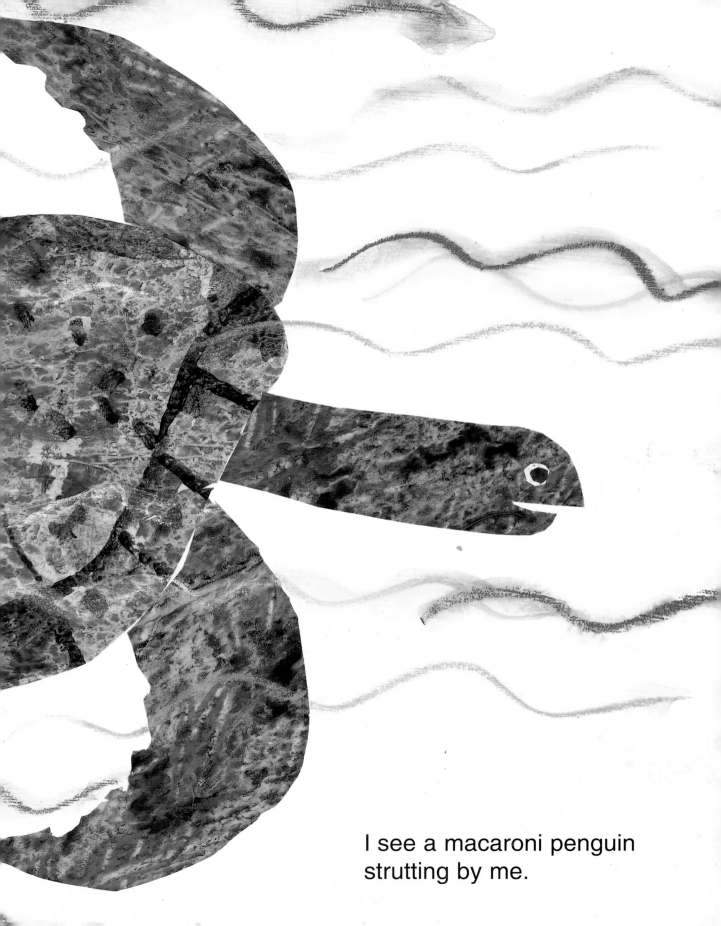

I see a macaroni penguin
strutting by me.

Macaroni Penguin,
Macaroni Penguin,
what do you see?

I see a sea lion
splashing by me.

Sea Lion,
Sea Lion,
what do you see?

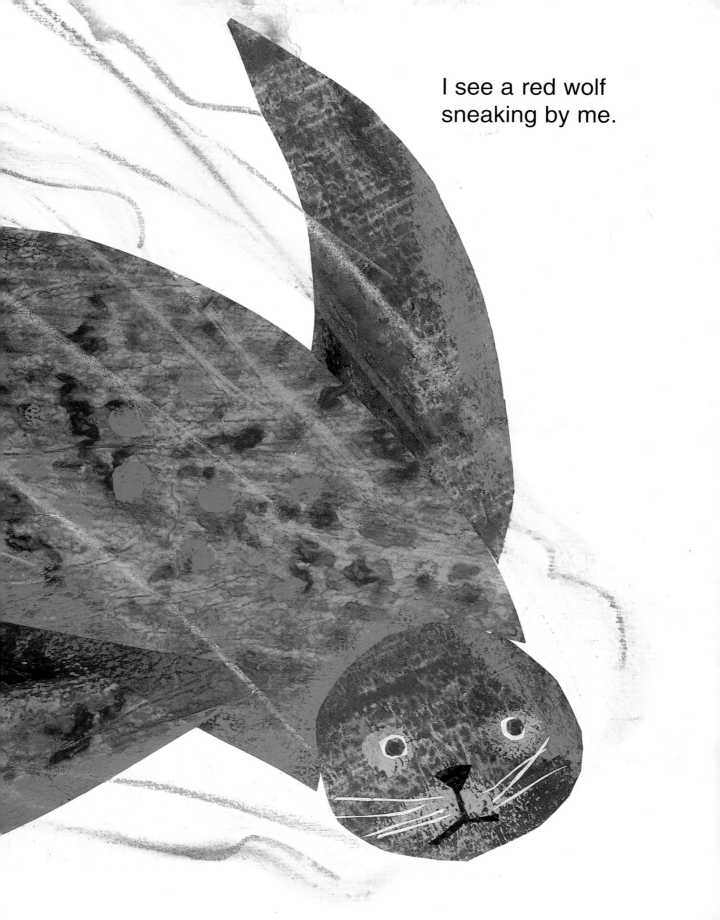

I see a red wolf
sneaking by me.

Red Wolf,
Red Wolf,
what do you see?

I see a whooping crane
flying by me.

Whooping Crane,
Whooping Crane,
what do you see?

I see a black panther
strolling by me.

Black Panther,
Black Panther,
what do you see?

I see a dreaming child
watching over me.

Dreaming Child,
Dreaming Child,
what do you see?

I see . . .

a panda bear,

a spider monkey,

a green sea turtle,

a red wolf,

a whooping crane,

a bald eagle,

a water buffalo,

a macaroni penguin,

a sea lion,

and a black panther . . .

**all wild and free –
that's what I see!**

Éric
Carle

Some other books by Eric Carle

The Very Hungry Caterpillar
ISBN 9780140569322

A small and very hungry caterpillar nibbles his way
through the pages of this classic book with die-cut pages
and finger-sized holes to explore.

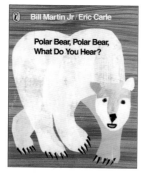

Polar Bear, Polar Bear, What Do You Hear?
ISBN 9780140545197

This playful story combines animals, colours and
sounds in a rowdy menagerie that children
will enjoy imitating.

Brown Bear, Brown Bear, What Do You See?
ISBN 9780140502961

Exuberantly coloured artwork and favourite animals
make this rhythmic story the perfect introduction
to looking and learning about colours.

The Mixed-Up Chameleon
ISBN 9780140506426

A story and game about a chameleon that suddenly
finds life exciting when it discovers it can change
not only its colour but its size and shape too.

The Bad-Tempered Ladybird
ISBN 9780140503982

The bad-tempered ladybird thinks she's bigger and better
than everyone else and picks fights with every animal she
meets, but she soon learns the importance of friends.